The Dangerous Captive

Steampunk OZ: Book 5

by Steve DeWinter

I0625877

Summary

In this action-packed second season of Steampunk OZ, American author S.D. Stuart returns to the Australis Penal Colony, where an ancient, and devastating, weapon was hidden a millennium ago.

Book 5

Imprisoned by the Southern Marshal, a half-human, half-lion hybrid lives behind an electrified fence with others like him. His only chance at freedom is to locate and recover an ancient weapon before a mysterious shadow organization uses it to conquer the world.

This book is a work of fiction. References to real people, events, establishments, organization, or locales are intended only to provide a sense of authenticity, and are used fictitiously. All other characters, and all incidents and dialogue, are drawn from the author's imagination and are not to be construed as real.

Ramblin' Prose Publishing

Copyright © 2014 Steve DeWinter

All rights reserved. Used under authorization.

www.stevedw.com

eBook Edition

ISBN-10: 1-61978-040-2

ISBN-13: 978-1-61978-040-8

Paperback Edition

ISBN-10: 1-61978-041-0

ISBN-13: 978-1-61978-041-5

Chapter 1

The Australis Penal Colony, the world's largest prison, seemed the most unlikely of places to hide something that could change the course of human events; but here Nero stood finally facing the end of his quest. The end of a long and bloody campaign that he almost lost to the brave defenders of this unmarked, and unremarkable, cavern along the northern coast of the Outcast Zone. Or as the locals called it, OZ.

The last of the defending soldiers held a skull sized rock over his head in one hand as he crouched over a small object on the ground in front of him. "If you take one step closer, I will destroy the key."

Nero smiled, but the scarring of his face caused by an explosion several months before, made it look more like a menacing scowl. "Give me the key and I will let you live."

The soldier looked past him to the motley crew of Nero's bloodied and battered soldiers. Less than three dozen remained of the 2,000 strong army that had set out from Central City under Nero's command four months earlier. "How do I know I can…"

His sentence was cut off by the blast from Nero's flintlock pistol, hidden deep in the folds of his cloak. The rock fell from the soldier's hand as he flopped to one side. He was dead before what was left of his head hit the ground.

Nero carefully lifted the six-inch long key from the ground. For the first time, since he had arrived in OZ decades earlier, he had what he needed to open the box. It was by pure chance he had obtained the key in the very same room as the box. Fortune was finally smiling on him.

He walked up to the large wooden box on the upraised stone pedestal at the center of the underground cavern.

He twirled the clockwork key around in his fingertips and studied the four concentric rings in the bow, the large grasping end of the key. The outermost ring was big enough to fill the palm of his hand. In addition, each individual ring had the entire twenty-four letter Greek alphabet stamped into the shiny brass.

As he spun each ring, the teeth on the other end moved back and forth, changing the shape of the key.

The key itself was a puzzle that needed to be solved before it would properly fit the warded lock of the wooden box that held a secret. A secret that would make those who had sent him to OZ establish themselves as masters over the entire world. But he had gotten to the box first, not them.

He spun the inner circle of the key around with his scarred thumb and noted the slight jump as it settled on each letter. He could not feel the resistance that preceded each letter because of the fried nerve endings caused when the fire had consumed his skin. Had he not landed in the fountain, when the explosion blew him from the top floor of his casino, he would have lost more than the sensation of touch.

The teeth of the key shifted as he spun the dial, lost in thought.

With only four rings, he was looking for a four letter Greek word to set the teeth in the correct positions. At least he was hoping it was a word that made sense. If it was just a four letter combination set randomly by the key's creator, there would be more than 330,000 possible permutations. Even if he was able to set the key and turn it in the lock once a minute for twenty-four hours a day, he could still be here for seven months before stumbling on the right combination.

He didn't have that kind of time. He'd already received word that the Directors were displeased with his performance and sending someone to replace him.

He had less than ten hours before his replacement arrived, which gave him less than ten hours to figure out the correct combination. Having a word that made sense would drastically reduce the time it took to find it. Knowing something about the creator of this key would also help narrow down the combination.

Nero stared at the key and back at the box.

The key only required four letters.

The answer had been staring him in the face the entire time.

He should've thought of this first. The ego of the lock's creator was about to betray his greatest secret.

Nero quickly spun the outer circle until the Greek letter "gamma" lined up with the cylindrical shaft of the key. He spun the next circle inward until the letter "alpha" lined up just to the right of gamma. He spun the next circle and lined up "lambda". He spun the innermost circle until he lined up the letter "epsilon" with the other letters to form the name of the creator of this particular puzzle lock.

GALE.

A solid click inside the internal mechanics of the key rewarded Nero with success. He gripped the key and slid it through the keyway on the front of the wooden box. He turned the key and it easily rotated in the lock for a quarter turn before it stopped and wouldn't turn any further. He twisted harder, but the key refused to budge.

The General, Nero didn't bother to learn their individual names, since he was the fifth soldier he had promoted to General since leaving Central City, pointed at the box and said in a cracking voice that betrayed his age of barely 16 years old. "Sir! The lock is bleeding."

Nero leaned in closer and saw the trickle of blood dripping from the lock. He removed his hand from the key and saw four drops of blood form quickly in the palm of his scarred hand. He inspected the key and saw the four needles protruding from the bow that fed the blood from the palm of his hand, through the shaft of the key, and into the lock. The fire that had taken his skin had also taken his ability to feel pain and he had not known the key had pierced him.

The anger grew quickly inside him, and it took all of his focus to stamp it back down before he erupted in a blind rage.

He closed his eyes and focused on his heartbeat until it slowed.

He took a deep breath and let it out slowly, allowing him to think more clearly.

Professor Benjamin Gale had done more than create a puzzle key to unlock this box. He had used his knowledge of genetics to program the lock to only open with his specific blood.

Nero had placed too much trust in the Professor. He had given him too much leeway as proof that he was doing the right thing, and now that was coming back to bite him. The Professor, and more recently, his daughter Dorothy, had been a thorn in his side for too long.

He regarded the large wooden box that refused to give up its secret. It looked like the Professor would be a thorn in his side for a little longer. The thing about thorns was, as long as it was stuck in your side you were fine. As soon as you removed it, you began to bleed.

Blood was the operative word here. He needed the Professor's blood to unlock this box. Since he had disappeared somewhere in OZ five years ago, Nero would have to use the next best thing. After all, she did share her father's genetics.

He contemplated taking an axe to the box. It was made of simple wood and would succumb easily to a sharpened blade. But destroying it might destroy the smaller object inside; and risk unleashing the greatest horror the world has ever known.

Nero looked over what remained of his army. There was no way he would be able to fight his way back to this cave if he left. There was only one option. He had to take the box to Dorothy, Professor Gale's daughter.

He removed the key from the lock and pulled it off of his hand. He inspected the sharp needles that protruded from the handle of the key. He could still see the traces of his blood that coated the sharpened tips. He spun the circles to withdraw the needles back into the handle before he slipped the key into his pocket. There were still more pieces of the puzzle he needed to collect before this key would open that box.

He addressed his nameless General. "Prepare the troops. We are heading home."

The General snapped to attention. "Yes sir!"

Nero strode over to his Chief Engineer, one of the few adults left in his dwindling army. "I am pretty sure that removing the box from the pedestal will trigger a trap."

The Engineer nodded. "From what we had to deal with just to get here, I wouldn't be surprised."

Nero was pleased he had found such a competent clockwork engineer in OZ. He didn't know what the man had done to be sent to OZ, and he didn't care. As long as he could safely remove the box from the pedestal, he was glad the man had done whatever he did on the outside.

The floor of the cave shuddered under Nero's feet and he struggled to remain standing. He heard a grating sound as if a massive rock was being scraped against another massive rock.

He instinctively glanced at the center of the cave and saw the General holding the box unsteadily in his arms with a perplexed look on his face as the pedestal lowered into the floor.

"What have you done!?" roared Nero.

At just barely thirteen years old, Jasper was the youngest member of Nero's army. He had been picking day-old dry chicken from his teeth when the whole cave began to tremble.

He snatched his blunderbuss, a large-caliber muzzle-loading weapon that must've been at least a hundred years old, off the ground and slung it over his shoulder. While he had been unsuccessful in actually hitting anything he shot at with the short-barreled firearm, it still looked menacing enough and could prove useful against anyone he came across on his way out of the crumbling cave.

With cracks forming in the roof of the cavern, he certainly was not going to stay in here any longer than he needed to.

Large chunks of rock dislodged from the ceiling and came crashing down, scattering his fellow soldiers in every direction.

A massive chunk of rock hit the ground right next to him so hard, it knocked him off his feet. He scrambled forward and began running for the exit.

He wasn't the only one. Everyone ran screaming through the collapsing cave toward the same small entrance that they had been forced to go through single file on their way in. If he wasn't one of the first ones through that opening, he might get stuck behind the clog of panicked bodies as everyone tried to get through.

Unfortunately, he had been one of the farthest from the exit, and it quickly jammed with soldiers trying to get out.

A terrified scream was cut short by a chunk of ceiling flattening another soldier.

Through the chaos he heard someone scream, "The box! Get the box!"

He quickly scanned the trembling chamber and found the box lying on its side next to a hole in the floor where the pedestal used to be. Leaving behind the whole reason they had come here in the first place seemed like a stupid thing to do. At the very least, he could sell it if he got it outside.

Screams of terror erupted from the entrance. He watched in horror as the walls of the thin tunnel that led out of the cavern slid closed, crushing the few who had already pushed their way into it.

He raced across the floor, keeping an eye on the ceiling above him as he dodged falling chunks of rock and slid to a stop next to the wooden box at the same time as the burnt old man. He was one of the few who knew that this old man was Nero, even though everyone thought Nero was dead. His troops had been told his name was Alexander.

His muscles tensed as he prepared to fight Nero for the box when Nero suddenly pushed it toward him.

He started to reach for the handles on the side of the box when Nero grabbed his wrist and shouted over the chaos. "I need you to tell me if this is a way out?"

He didn't have time to say anything before Nero shoved him head first into the hole. His stomach lurched as he fell into blackness. He reached out with his arms and legs and pressed against the walls of the tunnel to slow his descent. The tunnel walls were as smooth as glass and he couldn't slow himself down as he rocketed toward the unknown.

Even if he had seen it coming, and had taken a deep breath to prepare, when he hit the water at the bottom of the tunnel, it was so cold, it forced what little breath he had out of his lungs.

He somersaulted in the ice-cold water as the fast current pulled him along. He struggled to find which way was up until his head finally broke the surface. He gasped for air briefly before being pulled under again by the turbulent underground river.

He tumbled along alternating between holding what little oxygen he had in his lungs until they burned and gasping for quick breaths anytime he felt his face break the surface in the inky blackness.

If he had never taught himself how to swim in response to the village bully who, on a seemingly monthly basis, tied him into a burlap sack and threw him in the nearby lake, he would have drowned by now.

The trap, triggered by the removal of the box from the pedestal, had closed off the only entrance to the cave, but had opened a second. It was too risky to send the box down first without knowing if it was safe. Nero shoved the wooden box down the hole after he heard the kid splash into the river below. He never went into any enclosed space without first determining if there was another way out.

He ignored the terrified screams and cries for help all around him and instead focused on memorizing the face of the boy. Being able to recall that face perfectly would help him find the box again.

He took three deep breaths to force as much oxygen into his body and plunged headfirst into the hole, right before a massive chunk of ceiling crashed down on top of it, sealing the hole and the fate of those still alive in the cave.

They wouldn't be alive for much longer.

Chapter 2

Jasper hauled himself out of the icy water and onto the rocky shore. He had burst from the pitch black darkness and into the bright sun when the turbulent underground river became a fifty-foot waterfall that tossed him like yesterday's garbage into a small, but thankfully deep, lake.

At least this time he was not tied up inside a burlap sack and he quickly made his way to shore.

He removed the blunderbuss strapped to his back and stripped off the heavily soaked leather armor. He poured a gallon of water out of his blunderbuss when he tilted it upside down. His small bag of gunpowder was now a bag of black mud. It didn't matter, his blunderbuss had been too heavily dented from the fall, and from banging into rocks in the underground river, that it wouldn't be shooting anything ever again.

Something caught his eye and he focused on an object bobbing in the center of the lake. It was the wooden box. He took a deep breath and dove back into the lake.

He dragged the box up on the rocks and felt a chill run up his spine that had nothing to do with the temperature of the lake. He had developed his instinct for survival by growing up in the most dangerous place in the world. A continent sized prison was not the place for a boy of seven to be orphaned and alone on the streets. He had to grow up fast, and grow up fast he did.

His instincts had been sharpened to an almost supernatural level.

He glanced around him before he scanned the skies and spotted the black dot in the middle of the crisp blue sky that could mean only one thing. An airship was coming.

He dragged the box into a dense thicket of bushes halfway up the hill and had just returned to collect the leather armor and blunderbuss when he heard a loud splash at the base of the waterfall. He didn't bother looking because he knew what it meant. Somebody had followed him out of the cave.

He scrambled into the bushes and peered out as Nero clawed his way, coughing and sputtering, out of the water.

Nero flopped over onto his back and gulped in air for several minutes before he finally caught his breath and sat up.

Jasper crouched perfectly still in the bushes as he watched Nero look up and down the river and all around the waterfall and tiny lake. He held his breath every time Nero glanced in his direction for fear even the slightest movement of his chest expanding and contracting might shake the leaves and give away his hiding spot.

A shadow passed over the lake and settled on Nero, making him look up. Jasper craned his neck and saw an airship had already arrived and floated only a dozen feet above them.

Every airship he had seen before was slow and loud. It was why they were never useful in combat. Either the enemy saw them coming, heard them coming, or both, in plenty of time to prepare a proper defense. This one was different. It was long and sleek; and nimble. And it had come in silently on the wind.

He watched it spin around quickly to face windward and hold position without needing to be tethered to the ground. He could barely hear the propellers. And he was less than a hundred yards away.

He realized that the only reason he had seen it at all when he looked up into the bright blue sky was that it was painted a deep midnight blue with random white pinpoint dots all along the underside to match the night sky.

This airship was designed to sneak up on the enemy under cover of darkness. And it was not small. The long gondola that ran the entire length of the sleek airship could easily hold a hundred men.

He had never seen anything like it before and guessed that the owner would kill him immediately if he knew he was looking at it now.

The airship dropped to hover effortlessly ten feet off the ground. Nero stood defiantly facing the airship, not even attempting to run away. A ramp lowered from the front of the gondola. At the halfway point, the stairs along the ramp looked like the jagged teeth of a dingo, its gaping mouth threatening to swallow Nero whole. The ramp continued tilting downward until it settled lightly on the ground.

Jasper risked parting the branches of the bush wider to get a better look at the airship that floated rock steady in the shifting breeze without being tethered to the ground first. Even this close to the ground, the sound of the propellers could easily be dismissed as the slight rustling of leaves on some distant tree.

The adrenaline his body created while he fought for his life in the underground river was starting to dissipate and his body complained, with each lifting of the breeze, that he was still in wet clothing. To make matters worse, he had settled into a crouch in the bushes and his calf muscles were beginning to cramp. He had hoped to use the sound of the airship to mask his movement so he could sit down and relieve his leg muscles from their hunched stance, but this airship was too quiet. If he tried to reposition his legs to sit down, it might shift the loose rocks under his feet and Nero would hear him.

If Nero could hear him, so could the man walking down the ramp followed by a group of heavily armed soldiers.

For now, his muscles would just have to deal with the pain.

Nero stood there feeling like a drowned rat, and probably looking like one too, as Levi strode victoriously down the ramp like a conquering hero with his elite guard in tow. Every one of the nine-member guard was decked out in a modernized version of the armor worn by the Praetorian Guard, the personal bodyguards of Roman Emperors until they were disbanded in the fourth century, complete with crimson red heraldic crests mounted on top of their helmets.

Levi himself looked the part of an ancient Roman Emperor readying his troops for battle. The only thing missing was a laurel wreath on his head.

Nero did his best to stand up straight and appear stronger than he felt as he squinted up at Levi through the bright morning sun. "You're early."

Levi looked down his nose at him. "From the looks of you, it would appear I'm already too late. The Directors should have chosen me to come to this place instead of you."

Nero thrust his chin out defiantly. "I can only guess that it was you who convinced the Directors I needed to be replaced."

Levi frowned. "Take a look at yourself, Nero. Trust me when I tell you that it did not take much convincing."

"What makes you think you could have done any better?" Nero asked.

"Because I would have never cared about the natives," Levi replied as he held up a small device. "And I would have used one of these."

Nero shook his head. "It was buried under tons of rock; underground. That detector would never have led you to it."

Levi regarded the device in his hand. "The goddess of Rome sings, and this little toy can hear her."

"There is no goddess inside that box," Nero corrected him.

Levi smirked. "That's right. We live in an enlightened age. We are men of science. We don't care whether you call what's inside that box the evils of the world released by Pandora herself, or the God of the Hebrew's when they carried it around inside their ark, or even the Roman goddess Cybele, believed by the Oracle of Delphi to be encased in black meteoric stone. We don't believe that there is some mystical or magical being living inside the box. We believe that what is inside is quantifiable by science and ultimately controllable through scientific means."

Levi let out a sigh and looked down at Nero as if he were admonishing a small child. "I don't care who believes what it is. When the Hebrews had it, nations fell before them. When the Romans had it, they conquered their known world. Now the Directors want it, and they don't care how or why it does what it does. They only want it to do it for them."

"You are never going to find it with that thing."

"We'll see about that."

Levi flipped the switch on the detector and his face registered surprise. "If I am reading this correctly, it is very close."

Nero resisted the urge to glance at the bushes where the kid was most likely hiding with his box. When he first clamored out of the water, he noted the wet and overturned stones making a straight line from the water to the bushes. He had followed them both down the hole soon enough that there was no way he could have gotten any further. By the time Levi arrived and blathered on, the water had dried up enough that there was no visible indication anyone other than him had climbed out of the lake.

If he had any chance of keeping what was inside that box out of the Directors' hands, he had to convince Levi the box was not here.

He took a step toward Levi and paused when the two forward guards took a step toward him. "I pushed the box ahead of me down the hole right before the cave collapsed on my soldiers. If we leave now, we can catch up to it before it gets too far downriver and out of range of your detector."

Levi squinted at the device in his hand. "No. According to the gauge, when I walk this way the signal is stronger."

Nero took a sideways step and came between Levi and the bushes. "That's because your machine is detecting me."

Levi frowned at him. "What makes you say that?"

"When I fired a gun into my emerald laser to destroy it, the explosion embedded a piece of emerald shard inside me. Go ahead; wave your little trinket close to my chest."

Levi held the detector close to him and the needle on the gauge jumped.

Nero breathed a silent sigh of relief. He hadn't known whether the emerald shard would interfere with the detector or not. "This river goes by a town less than three kilometers from here. If someone else spots that box floating in the river and fishes it out, it will be even harder to retrieve."

Levi smiled. "I highly doubt that. I have an armada of a hundred airships, just like this one, due to hit the northern coast within a week. If we have not recovered the box within that time, my army of ten thousand soldiers will tear this place apart until we do."

Jasper's legs trembled under the strain of not having moved while he stayed in a half-crouched position in the middle of the bushes. Nero glanced back in his direction and gave a slight nod just before he disappeared up the ramp into the airship.

He overheard everything the man talking to Nero had said. He also remembered Nero's earlier comment about the detector not working if the box was underground.

It wouldn't take them long before they realized the box had not gone down the river. They would ignore anything Nero tried to tell them and return here to begin their search.

If he wasn't gone by then, they would most likely kill him when they took the box. He had overheard the invasion plans for OZ and they would not leave any witnesses behind who could potentially warn somebody.

He had to get away from this place as quickly as possible if he hoped to live to see another sunrise. He had no idea where to go. He had never traveled into the Northern Territories before Nero led his army here to retrieve the box.

He had to hide it somewhere where it could not be detected by that device, and before anyone saw him with it.

Suddenly, the box felt heavier as he dragged it up the hill and away from the river.

Chapter 3

For the first time in his life, Caleb was around others just like him. The entire town was filled exclusively with half-human half-animal hybrids and, when he walked through the market in town, he was greeted with smiles rather than gasps of horror because he looked more lion than human.

The Southern Marshal had broken years of silence and separatism to offer sanctuary for every hybrid in OZ. Eager to escape the persecution they suffered at the hands of humans, they accepted her offer and, for the first time in a decade, outsiders crossed the thousand-foot high ceramic wall that separated the Southern Territories from the rest of OZ.

When the last airship crossed over the wall, the border was closed again and all contact with the outside world was severed. The Southern Marshall had provided a safe harbor for the hybrids. She had even gone so far as to build an entire town specifically for them. A place where they could live in peace and harmony. And then she surrounded it with a fifty-foot tall electrified fence.

Officially, the fence was to keep out those who wanted to harm the hybrids. But Caleb knew deep down in his soul, the fence was really there to keep them in. He didn't know why and he didn't care to know why. He didn't like to be caged up, regardless of the reason.

He was finding it difficult to shift from being Nero's personal bodyguard and assassin to becoming the leader, by birthright, of the hybrid compound.

Everything was better inside the compound. The hybrids were not persecuted for being different and, as their leader, his word was law. As the ruler over this tiny kingdom, he could have anything he wanted. But the thing he wanted most was to leave.

Every morning he woke up with a list of royal obligations, things he needed to do as the king of his people. Yet every morning always ended the same way. With him looking out through the fence toward a freedom he might never attain again.

This was not to say he had never gone over the fence.

No prison, not even OZ itself, had ever been able to contain him. Despite always being able to leave, he always managed to return of his own free will. Maybe it was not so much free will as it was a sense of obligation. He returned to OZ, when he was younger, out of his obligation to Nero for rescuing him from death. He returned to the compound out of his obligation to the hybrid community, who saw him as their natural-born leader.

Whatever it was that always brought him back, he knew there was one person he would be willing to leave everything for and never once look back. But he had lost her the same day they climbed over that wall into the Southern Territories. It had been six months since they were captured and separated. Six long months of not knowing whether she was alive or dead.

Not a single one of the informants he'd cultivated outside the fence had brought him any word about her. It was as if she ceased to exist the moment she was taken away from him, and he was losing his grip on the hope that she was still alive.

He closed his eyes and tried to picture her face. It was getting harder each day, the details blurring into generalities under the relentless march of time. Imbalanced by the memory of all he had lost, he leaned in too close to the electrified wire fence, causing tufts of fur to lift up from his skin and stretch out in the direction of freedom. He ignored the smell of burning fur as some of the longer strands came in contact with the wire.

"You know, there are safer ways to cut your hair to a respectable length."

His eyes snapped open and he regained his balance as he leaned back away from the fence.

Zee held a finger to her nose to block out the smell. She was one of the few hybrids that looked almost entirely human. If it weren't for the soft coat of white fur with black striping over her entire body, she would never have been sent to live behind the fence.

"If you keep looking out that fence, you'll miss everything we have in here."

"We are caged in here like wild animals."

"The fence is for our safety."

"Safety from what?"

"You were sheltered from what the rest of us had to deal with, out there in the real world. We were second class citizens… no, third class citizens. We were not allowed in schools. We were not allowed to have jobs. The lucky ones were given menial and dehumanizing chores that just barely kept the rest of the family in poverty."

He reached for the fence with a hand and stopped himself short of touching it. He could feel the warmth emanating off the wire.

"There has to be a better way than this."

"I agree with you Caleb, but for most of us here this is the best we have ever had. Out there I worked as a sideshow attraction in a traveling circus. In here, I'm being taught clockwork engineering. If I test well this season, I might be one of the five taken this year to the Southern Marshal's private university for further training."

The wind kicked up and jostled the fence, the wire almost touching his outstretched palm. He lowered his hand and looked at her. "Have you asked yourself why, Zee?"

"Why what?"

"Why has the Southern Marshal taken such an interest in us?"

"I've learned not to question good fortune. She has given all of us more than she has taken away."

He looked back through the fence. "Not all of us."

She placed a hand on his shoulder. "You miss her, don't you?"

"I think I shall never see her again."

"I wouldn't write her off that easily."

"It's been six months without a word."

"I wouldn't say that," she said as she held up a small slip of paper.

He stared at the yellow stained paper gripped between two fingers.

"What is that?"

"Your word."

He reached for the paper and she withdrew it back quickly. "Don't jeopardize everything we have been given here for her."

She offered it to him again and he snatched it out of her hand. "I just have to know that she's safe."

Fifteen kilometers from the hybrid compound, in the middle of one of the busiest trading cities in the Southern Territories, Darius, only sixteen years old but already showing signs that his hair pattern was following the family trait, paced back and forth in the back room of Uncle Jedediah's small cottage.

Jedediah sat calmly at the kitchen table with his arms crossed over his enormous belly. "Stop being so nervous Nephew or your head will be as bald and shiny as mine before you're twenty. Relax, he will be here soon."

Darius gestured in the air with his arms as he spoke. "The Marshal has a twenty-four hour curfew on all government workers. If

I'm caught outside the relay station like this, I'll be killed on the spot as a spy."

"Relax. You'll be back before the lunchtime roll call."

"Are you sure about that?"

"Money doesn't buy happiness, but it does buy silence. Your share of the reward is more than enough to cover the costs to keep your little transgression from the ears of the Marshal."

Darius let out a long steadying breath. "I sure hope you're right Uncle."

A knock at the front door stirred Jedediah from his chair. "That would be him now. You stay back here while I talk to him for a minute first."

Darius grabbed Jedediah's sleeve. "Get the money up front."

Jedediah patted his cheek and smiled. "That's what I'm going to talk about. You just wait here."

Darius held his breath as he listened to his uncle unlatch the front door. In a few minutes he would tell the stranger what he knew, collect his reward and head back to the relay station before the Southern Marshal's security forces even knew he was gone.

He snuck out from the relay station on an almost weekly basis just to get away from the structured schedule of a government employee. He wasn't the only one who snuck away, and they always covered for each other. Life could get pretty boring when you were young and vibrant, and stuck in a dead-end job. Sneaking out to enjoy the nightlife of the nearest city was almost a requirement. If you didn't do it, you were most likely a snitch for upper management.

But this was the first time he had broken an emergency curfew to sneak out in the light of day. It was far riskier than sneaking out at night, and he hoped his coworkers would be able to cover for him long enough to collect his reward and get back before he was missed. Even after he paid them all off, he would end up with more money in one night than he had been able to save from his meager salary over the previous ten years of dedicated service.

Tonight's influx of cash might even put him over the top and enable him to pay off the family debt. A shiver ran up his spine as he thought of the possibility that the entire family could actually leave their government jobs behind and finally be able to look for work in the much more lucrative private sector. Maybe even take his first vacation since he began working fifty-hour weeks as a six-year-old boy.

The iron hinges groaned softly as the front door opened partway, followed immediately by a loud crash and a sharp cry from his uncle.

Darius heard several heavy boots rush into the front room followed by a commanding voice. "Where is he?"

"I don't know who…" was all he heard his uncle could say before there was a gunshot.

Darius glanced around him quickly. This couldn't be the stranger they were waiting for. His uncle had met the stranger a few times before and said that he was always polite and sincere. And always alone.

It could only mean one thing. He had been discovered missing from the government barracks and the Southern Marshal sent out her soldiers to track him down and kill him.

But how had they found him so quickly? He was certain he had not been followed on foot and he would have seen or heard any airships in the sky. Why didn't the lookouts on the outskirts of town warn anyone that soldiers were coming?

Somehow, the soldiers had made it all the way to the center of town without triggering the active underground movement that seemed to know everything that took place in the city right before it happened.

Unfortunately, he didn't have time to worry about how the soldiers had found him. The truth of the matter was, they had found him. The only thing he had time to worry about was how to get away.

The sound of boots rushing down the hallway from the front room sent him into action. Doors were kicked open followed by shouts of the word "clear" all along the hallway as the soldiers got closer to the kitchen.

He reached for the lock on the back door and froze as his heart jumped into his throat. The door handle was already being turned by somebody on the other side. All the commotion at the front of the house had masked the noise of soldiers approaching the back door. Now that he was focused on it, he could hear someone curse when the handle bumped against the lock and prevented whoever was on the other side from opening the door.

It didn't matter who was on the other side. Darius could not escape through the back door, and the soldiers were about to enter the kitchen from the front hallway.

The small window over the sink darkened as someone peered in through the thick brown grime that covered the glass.

There were only three ways out of the kitchen. The hallway, the back door, and the window over the sink. And there were soldiers at every one of them. He was trapped with nowhere to go.

He was about to be caught and put to death as a spy. With the added fine levied against every relative of an executed spy, his family would never be able to work off the debt. Not even if they each lived to be five hundred years old. Because of his attempt to make some quick cash to clear the family debt, his entire family's future, even those who had not been born yet, had suddenly gone up in smoke.

The basic instinct of survival kicked in and his eyes focused on the hearth in the corner of the kitchen. Up in smoke, he thought again. Or more likely, up with smoke.

Living a life in governmental servitude meant not getting very much to eat. One of the benefits was that you stayed very skinny.

Maybe even skinny enough to fit up a chimney flue at sixteen years old.

The soldiers rushed in from the hallway just as the other group of soldiers broke through the back door. They all spilled into the kitchen at exactly the same time that Darius pulled his feet up into the chimney, and out of sight.

"The rest of the house is empty," someone shouted.

"Nobody left out the back door. It was even locked from the inside when we got to it," another voice said.

"I saw someone in here when I looked through the window," a third voice said.

Darius climbed quietly up the chimney as he silently prayed that there were no loose stones for him to dislodge and send crashing back down into the kitchen.

The chimney became smaller as he climbed and he had to exhale deeply and take smaller breaths to keep from becoming wedged in the ever shrinking flue.

As he neared the top, it had become so thin he had to keep his arms above his head. His knees had less room to bend as he climbed. He felt the sudden rush of wind on his fingers as his hands passed the threshold of the top of the chimney.

He was almost out.

He took a small breath and felt the chimney constrict him on all sides like a snake.

His hands gripped the top of the chimney flue, but he had no leverage to pull himself up because he couldn't bend his arms. He tried to push himself up with his feet, but the flue prevented his legs from bending and the toes of his shoes lost their grip on the charcoal dusted stones. The only thing that kept him from falling all the way back down into the kitchen, and into the gun sights of the waiting soldiers, was the involuntary breath that expanded his chest and held him in place.

He held his breath and struggled to find purchase again with this toes. While his feet frantically searched for a small crevice to wedge the toes of his shoes into, his lungs burned with the desire to exhale so they could take another tiny breath of soot choked air. He felt like he was drowning in one of the driest places in the world. But if he exhaled before his feet found something to hold on to he would slide down the chimney, making all kinds of noise as he scrambled to stop himself.

Right before his body overrode his conscious desire to keep holding his breath, his toes found a crevice and wedged themselves in just as he blew out the bad air from his lungs.

He exhaled so sharply, he dislodged some of the soot clinging to the sides of the chimney and sucked in the tiny black cloud when he gasped his next breath.

His body involuntarily coughed before he could hold his breath to stop it.

From below he heard someone exclaim, "Did you hear that?"

Panic gripped him tighter than the chimney.

With his body in the way, he couldn't see down the chimney at the face that was probably looking up at him by now. But there was no mistaking the next thing he heard.

"The kid went up the chimney."

Hands grabbed his wrists above him and, not wanting to spend any more time stuck in the chimney than he needed to, he exhaled sharply as someone yanked him out the top.

Chapter 4

Before the staccato of gunfire had erupted in the sleepy little trading village, Caleb had been standing under the same intersection road sign for the third time and staring at the yellow scrap of paper that held the address of where to meet his contact. Most of the cities in OZ grew organically and the streets were twisty and seemingly random. He longed for the ordered and logical layout of Little Roma, Nero's meticulously planned city in the Eastern Territories, were he grew up.

When a single shot echoed through the streets, his feline senses zeroed in on the direction of the gunshot, despite the numerous echoes it created around the haphazardly constructed city.

He had broken out in a fast run in the direction of trouble.

It had been pure luck he saw soot-covered hands poking out of the chimney that matched the address on his piece of paper.

He had leapt up onto the roof in a single bound and yanked a boy out of the chimney. Before he had a chance to ask the boy if the man he was supposed to meet was still alive, soldiers rushed into the street and pointed rifles up at him.

He tackled the boy just as bullets ricocheted off the chimney, and together, they tumbled off the roof.

It's not true, what they say. Cats don't always land on their feet.

He gripped the boy tightly to cushion the fall with his own body as they fell backward into a massive pile of rotting vegetables and garbage. The pile wasn't as thick as he hoped and the impact knocked the wind out of him. His body begged to lay there for a moment to recover as he forced himself back to his feet and scanned the alley for anything he could use as a weapon.

There was nothing but wilted lettuce, stale bread, and apple cores all around him. Not even a plank of wood he could wield like a club.

Angry shouts echoed from both ends of the alleyway. There was no way out except the way they had come in.

Caleb pulled the boy out of the garbage and gripped his shoulders. "Have you ever run along the rooftops and jumped from one building to another?"

The boy nodded his head.

Caleb grabbed the scruff on the back of the boy's shirt with one hand and gripped his pants at the waist with the other. "As soon as you are on the roof, start running and don't stop."

The boy cried out in surprise as Caleb tossed him back up onto the roof. Caleb crouched and faced the closer entrance to the alley just as a soldier rushed around the corner. His leg muscles exploded with raw power as he pounced and leaped nine feet through the air. The soldier froze with a look of terror on his face. Caleb knocked him to the ground hard enough to render the soldier unconscious and liberated his rifle from him.

He spun around just as soldiers rushed in from the other end of the alley. Caleb lifted the rifle and squeezed the trigger several times, with the first pull firing the rifle before jamming. One soldier went down while the rest scrambled back out of the alley. He fiddled with the trigger, but really didn't have time to deal with a jammed rifle, so he dropped it and hopped up onto the roof. He wasn't going to wait around for the soldiers to regroup and storm the alley. A mere second of hesitation was equal to a lifetime of poor decisions when it came to battle strategy. They always resulted in an untimely death for the person who made them.

A natural hunter, Caleb immediately spotted the boy cresting the roof of a house several streets away. He took off after him and had leaped across to a third roof when he saw a large shadow pass over the roof of the house to the left of the boy, heading in the same direction he was.

Caleb slid to a stop on the tile roof and scanned the skies for the airship that was tracking the boy.

He saw nothing.

He heard nothing.

The sky was bright blue and clear, except for a few clouds in the distance. The boy crested the roof of another building and kept running until he dipped back out of sight again. Caleb watched the massive shadow darken the roof as it moved into position right behind him.

Caleb searched the sky again, looking for whatever was casting that shadow. But there was nothing. And then a strange thing happened. Some of the blue sky crossed in front of one of the distant clouds. He squinted at the misplaced section of sky as it crossed in front of the cloud and then blended back in with the rest of the sky on the other side.

If he had not seen it with his own eyes, he would never have believed it. He didn't know if the unendurable stress of life behind the fence had finally gotten to him, or if he'd actually seen an airship painted the color of the sky.

The kid crested another rooftop with the shadow nipping at his heels. Whatever it was, it was gaining on the kid.

Gliding silently above the city in her new airship, courtesy of the man who called himself Levi and who was now a guest in her dungeon, the Southern Marshal held the spyglass steady as she watched her prey run helplessly along the rooftops.

"Don't let him get away. He will be an example for the others."

Taylor, the captain of her private guard, cleared his throat behind her. Without taking her eyes off her prey she said, "What is it, Captain?"

"The forward team has reported in. One suspect is dead and they are pursuing a second suspect on foot. We have already suffered a casualty at the hands of the second suspect."

Without taking her eye off the spyglass she replied, "Tell them to focus their efforts on apprehending the second suspect. Even if he is just some good Samaritan who just happened to be in the wrong place at the wrong time, he will answer for killing one of my men."

"Yes ma'am. And the boy?"

"I wouldn't worry too much about him. He's about to run out of roofs to jump across."

Darius skidded to a stop on the edge of the roof and gazed out at the open field that spread out before him on either side. He had reached the edge of town and there was nowhere else to go. The low grasslands that stretched to the horizon offered no place to hide. His only hope was to drop down into the city, work his way through the narrow streets, and avoid anyone who might be looking for him.

A massive shadow crawled up the roof and settled all around him, the temperature dropping several degrees in the shadow of…what? He looked up into the clear blue sky; and could not find the sun.

A patch of the sky a shade darker than the rest, with a glow emanating from its edges, was getting bigger. Whatever had swallowed up the sun was expanding to swallow up the entire sky.

No, he suddenly realized with a chill that trickled up his spine. Whatever it was that ate the sun wasn't getting bigger, it was getting closer.

A portion of the sky peeled away, like someone drawing back the curtain on a window, to reveal the hatch of an airship. He could see that he wasn't looking at the sky at all, but canvas sails painted the same color as the sky. Now that he knew what he was looking at, he could make out the numerous strips of canvas, which covered the entire underside of the airship, rippling in the wind.

He stood on the roof, transfixed by the skill and mastery involved with camouflaging an entire airship. But how had they managed to mask the sound of the propellers? While his mind struggled to comprehend the mechanical marvel that hovered above him, he failed to notice the hatch slide open and rope lines drop down. The knotted ends hit the tile of the roof with a loud smack and jarred him out of his shocked stupor.

His head snapped in the direction of the sudden sound and his eyes focused on the rope. He tilted his head up and saw men, armed men, rappelling down the rope toward him. His mouth went dry and his skin broke out in a cold sweat.

Several roofs away, the cat man ran toward him, shouting something. From this far away, he couldn't hear what the cat man was saying clearly, but he understood perfectly what he meant.

Get off the roof and keep running.

Darius clambered to the edge of the roof and peaked over. His muscles relaxed slightly with relief when he saw the large haystack along the side of the house. He didn't waste any time looking back and jumped.

His shirt tugged tightly against his throat and yanked him backward to slam him against the side of the house. His shirt collar was choking him as he flailed around, suspended fifteen feet off the ground.

He clawed in a panic at his shirt. He must've somehow caught it on the edge of the roof, and now it was cutting off his air supply. He reached up to unhook his shirt from whatever it had caught on, and felt the meaty hand of the soldier.

The soldier hauled him back up onto the roof and tossed him down with a curse. He shoved his boot deep into Darius' back, keeping him flat on his stomach. "The little bugger nearly wrenched my arm out of its socket."

The other soldier pointed his rifle at Darius while addressing his comrade in arms. "That was an excellent catch. I thought you were going to go over with him."

Darius lifted his head and scanned the nearby roofs, but the cat man was gone. When he first pulled him out of the chimney, he thought the cat man had rescued him from certain death. Now he knew he only delayed the inevitable.

And now, when he needed him most, the cat man had abandoned him to his fate.

Caleb had seen the soldiers rappelling down the rope and capturing the boy. He dropped off the next roof and would have to travel the rest of the way on the ground if he had any hope of sneaking up on the soldiers before they took what might be his only connection to finding Dorothy.

There were way too many dead-end streets in this town, and it took longer than he wanted to arrive at the house with the airship hovering above the roof. It gave his unknown enemy more time to mount a proper defense, or just plain leave, before he got there.

He peeked around the building that was right next to his target. He used the large shadow, which engulfed the streets surrounding the building, to let him know where the airship was. The same way you would use the tracks of a white rabbit left behind in a snowy field to know where the rabbit was.

He effortlessly leaped fifteen feet straight up and grabbed the edge of the roof above him. Using his momentum he vaulted himself up onto the roof and landed with a soft thud. Above him, at the top of the slanted roof, a soldier stood with his back to him. Caleb crouched low and slowly ascended the roof toward the soldier.

A loose terra-cotta tile dislodged under his foot, clattering down the roof and over the edge.

The soldier spun around, saw Caleb, and raised his gun to fire off a shot. Time slowed to a snail's crawl and Caleb could see the disturbed air ripple outward as the bullet tore through the atmosphere. The bullet's shock wave tickled the tuft of fur at the tip of Caleb's ear as it whizzed past, missing him by a mere centimeter.

The soldier abruptly yanked the lever of his repeating rifle, ejecting the spent cartridge and loading a new one into the chamber of the barrel. In less than half a second, he would be ready to fire on Caleb again. If the soldier had barely missed him on such a hasty targeting opportunity, he would never miss if given the chance to sight down his barrel properly at Caleb.

Caleb wasn't about to give him that chance. He charged forward and let out a mighty roar. The soldier took an instinctive step backward and slipped on a loose tile himself. He did the splits before falling backward off the ridge of the roof and disappearing from view.

Caleb scrambled to the top of the roof and looked over the ridge just in time to see the soldier slide down on his back and drop over the edge head first. His scream was cut off moments later by a sickening splat that sounded like a watermelon splitting open when dropped on a stone floor.

Caleb heard numerous shouts all around him. The noise drew everyone's attention right to Caleb.

Around him, soldiers pointed their rifles at him from nearby rooftops.

Darkness engulfed the entire roof where he stood. The part of the sky above him blocked out the sun. Soldiers had already jumped over from the nearby rooftops and were approaching him from every direction. There was nowhere he could run. There was no way he could fight. He was outnumbered and outgunned.

The only thing to do was surrender.

Caleb held his arms high and complied with every order barked at him until he lay face down on the rooftop with his hands bound behind his back.

Within moments, he felt the tug on the bindings around his hands that pulled him slowly up to a standing position and then kept going, lifting him off the roof. His shoulders strained to support his entire weight as he was pulled up into the waiting airship.

Chapter 5

Caleb didn't struggle when hands grabbed him and pulled him into the airship. He let the soldiers manhandle him as they untied the rope used to haul him up and then left him face down on the polished hardwood floor of the airship's gondola.

A deep baritone voice spoke. "What have we got here, Lieutenant?"

"It appears a hybrid has broken out of the compound, Captain."

Caleb recognized the deeper voice, the one the lieutenant called Captain, as the same man who led the team that had captured him and Dorothy as soon as they came over the southern wall.

He craned his neck to see the Captain's face and made direct eye contact with him.

He was right. This was the same man who had taken her. He had vowed to himself that, the next time he saw this man, he would make him suffer greatly for separating them. But he had not expected to be tied up and lying face down when that time came. Instead of doing everything he'd always dreamed of doing to this man, all he could do was stare at him.

"Where is Dorothy?" he growled.

The Captain looked down at his captive and frowned. "We didn't just catch any hybrid. We caught the king of the beasts."

Caleb struggled against his bindings. It only resulted in a boot being placed on his back by another soldier to hold him down.

"Where is Dorothy?" Caleb growled again.

The Captain knelt down. "You're like a phonograph cylinder with only one recording. Where's Dorothy? Where's Dorothy?"

He tugged on Caleb's whiskers, causing tears to well up in the corners of his eyes from the excruciating pain. "A couple of hours with me and I can teach you to say a few more human words."

A female voice behind the Captain interrupted him. "That'll be enough, Captain Taylor."

Taylor immediately snapped to attention. "Yes ma'am."

The pain in his whiskers subsided and Caleb's eyes focused on the Southern

Marshal. She shook her head at him like a mother shaking her head at a child caught with his hand in the cookie jar. "Lift him up."

Strong hands grabbed his bound arms from behind and brought him quickly to his feet.

The Southern Marshal let out a sigh. "When my young wireless operator broke curfew, I followed him expecting to uncover a vast spy network operating within the confines of my territory. I did not expect to find you."

"I didn't…" A soldier punched him in the stomach, cutting him off. He doubled over and coughed and sputtered, the wind knocked out of him. The other soldier yanked on his mane and brought his head back up. Caleb could smell the tang of onions on the soldier's breath as he spoke. "The Marshal did not ask you a question. You will not speak until directed to do so."

The Southern Marshal's eyes became slits while she most likely pondered what to do with him. She had apparently made up her mind when she opened her mouth to speak. "Tell me something, Caleb. What did you offer my employees that made them willing to spy on me in my own kingdom?"

"Only if you tell me something first," Caleb replied.

The soldier who had punched him a moment ago reared back, ready to slam his balled fist into Caleb's solar plexus again. She held up her hand and stopped him.

They both stared quietly at each other for a long drawn-out moment before she finally responded. "She is alive and well."

Caleb's heart fluttered with excitement. "I want to see her."

"I've answered your question. Now answer mine."

Caleb tugged against the soldiers who held him in place. "Let me see her!"

"Answer my question!"

"I offered them a reward for any information they could find on Dorothy."

"You offered them money?"

"Yes."

"And they willingly spied for you? For money?"

He shook his head. "No. They did not spy for me. I only wanted information about

Dorothy. I told them I was not interested in anything that didn't directly relate to finding her."

"And what exactly did you offer as a reward?"

"One thousand sovereigns."

She let out a surprised laugh. "And just how did you expect to follow through on your promise? I don't recall allowing any money into the hybrid compound."

She glanced over at Captain Taylor. "Did he have any money on him when you captured him at the wall?"

Taylor shook his head.

She regarded Caleb with a quizzical look. "How did you expect to follow through with your promise of a reward?"

He lowered his head. "We saw the soldiers coming while we were still halfway down the wall. As soon as we hit ground, I buried the money I brought with me before we set up the small camp, well away from my hiding spot, where your soldiers captured us."

"How much did you bring with you?"

Caleb stared at his shoes. The soldier grabbed a fistful of mane again and pulled his head up.

"How much did you bring?" she repeated.

"Five thousand sovereigns."

Her eyebrows lifted in surprise. "You don't pack light, do you? That was nearly forty kilograms of gold."

Caleb was shocked at how quickly she had calculated the total weight.

"You determined the weight of all those coins in your head?"

"I'm not the Southern Marshal because I'm pretty."

Caleb smirked. "But it doesn't hurt that you're pretty."

That remark got him another punch to the gut, but it was worth it.

Unfazed, the Southern Marshal tilted her head at him. "I'm just impressed you made it over the wall at all."

Caleb rolled his shoulders with the memory of the heavy pack, but it was time to get this conversation back on track.

"I answered your questions. Now when can I see her?"

"You may see her as soon as we get back to my castle, but only on one condition."

"And what is that?"

"You fulfill your destiny and become a leader to your people."

Caleb dropped his shoulders and let out a big sigh. "They're not my people."

"Of course they are. Just because you were raised apart from them does not make you no longer one of them. They want to look up to you, Caleb. They want you to be their leader. I want you to be their leader."

Caleb reflected on her final statement. That was the one thing that did not make sense. Why was she taking such an interest in the hybrids? Why had she given them refuge from the persecution throughout OZ, only to place them behind an electrified fence and make them captives inside a prison within a prison?

He just couldn't believe she did all this out of the goodness of her heart. She had to have some angle, some reason. And somehow her focus had fallen on him.

"Why do you want me to be their leader?"

"When I sent out the call that I was offering a haven for hybrids, they came from all over OZ. Not just some of them. All of them came. I gathered a scattered and broken people from the four corners of the Outcast Zone and brought them together, save for one."

"Me."

"You were the only one I could not reach with my message. And you were the son of the king and queen that ruled the hybrid kingdom before it was targeted and destroyed by humans. The humans were afraid. Afraid that, given the chance, hybrids could come to rule all of OZ. So they obliterated your kingdom and scattered the hybrids to the winds, enacting laws that kept the status of hybrids just barely that above the livestock in the fields."

He had heard the same tale from Zee many times before.

"You haven't answered my question."

"I have given the hybrids everything that humans took away from them. I gave them a place where they could live without persecution. I've made education available to every one of them. But there was one thing that I could not restore."

"Their kingdom."

"At least not without their king."

He was beginning to understand why she believed him to be integral to what she had planned for the hybrids. But what did she have planned?

He gazed into the deep black abyss of her eyes. They glistened back, but refused to reveal any of her secrets.

"You want me to be a leader to my people?"

Her face softened as she smiled. "I want you, to want to be a leader for your people."

"What's the difference?"

"If you do what I want, you do it with your head. When you do what you want, you do it with your heart."

"Why is this so important to you?"

She reflected on his question for a moment before finally answering. "It's not just important to me. It's important to you, to every hybrid, and to every human in OZ. Your decision to finally become a leader just might matter to the entire world."

A voice he vaguely recognized from his past spoke from behind him. "She's right, Caleb."

The speaker of the new voice stepped into his view, and his heart leapt into his throat. Despite the lack of hair, and intense scarring over the entire face of the man standing before him, he recognized him in an instant.

"Nero?"

The horribly scarred face grimaced in an attempt to smile. "How are you doing, son?"

Caleb lurched forward, but was held back by the two guards who gripped his arms tightly. "You are not my father!"

Nero leaned heavily on the cane he clutched in one hand. "So much for time heals all wounds."

"I should've known you would be behind this. The puppet master pulling on all the strings."

Nero let out a guttural chuckle. The damage to his body, when the emerald laser had exploded and ejected him out the window of the casino, was far more than skin deep and consigned a deeper, raspier, quality to his voice.

He motioned toward the Southern Marshal with a swish of his cane. "I'm afraid this time, she's the one in charge. I'm only here to help."

"Help!? Since when have you been the one they call when someone needs help?"

"Actually, I came to her. To ask for her help."

Caleb practically choked on his own laugh.

"Okay, similar question. Since when have you needed help from anyone?"

"For the first time, something is coming that even I, with my vast resources and connections, cannot take on alone."

"And just what is it that has the two of you, the most powerful people in all of OZ, running and hiding with your tail between your legs?"

Nero coughed to clear his throat. "They are the people who sent me here to find something for them."

"Who are 'they'?"

Nero shook his head. "The infamous 'they' go by the name of the Directors. A small group of world leaders that operate in the shadows. I think there are only five members at any given time who make all the decisions."

The Southern Marshal interrupted him. "You think? Don't you know? Aren't they the ones who sent you here?"

Nero nodded. "They only speak through proxies. I was given my instructions without ever meeting them in person."

The Southern Marshal apparently wasn't going to let this drop. "You've been working all this time for somebody you've never met? How can you even be sure they exist?"

He cleared his throat again and did not look directly into the eyes of the Southern

Marshal. Instead, he found something very interesting on the floor at his feet while he spoke. "The Directors do exist, Madame Marshal, believe me. And the threat they pose is very real."

Caleb had never seen Nero behave like this. Even when he wasn't at the forefront, and hung back in the shadows, Nero always made sure that everyone around him knew who was really in charge. Now, for the first time, Caleb saw him for what he really was. Or at least what he had become. A broken man who was powerless to take what he wanted by force and had no choice but to supplicate himself to another.

She folded her arms across her chest and gave Nero a stern look. "You've got me all worked up over nothing."

For the briefest of moments, Caleb saw a flash of the old Nero as he matched the Southern Marshal's stare with one of his own. "It is hardly nothing. The dragons are coming to destroy everything we hold dear. We have to work together if we are to stop them."

Chapter 6

Caleb was taken down below the main deck, chained to the wall in a small room, and left alone. He was actually glad to be given this time to think. After the guard closed the door and left him some privacy, Caleb tugged on the chains. They were securely bolted to the support beam along the wall. Even if he did manage to break free, where could he go? He was on an airship, hundreds of meters in the sky.

And even if he managed to escape an airship in mid-flight, and make it safely to the ground, where could he go then?

A hybrid wandering around the Southern Territories, outside of electrified the fence, would cause quite a stir in any town or city he entered. He certainly didn't want to live out the rest of his days as a wild animal, living deep in some forest hunting for his food and hiding from everything else.

He couldn't escape back into the rest of OZ either. The ceramic wall that surrounded the Southern Territories was as smooth as glass and dwarfed the tallest trees. The tools he had used to get in had been confiscated when they were captured. And besides, he still had to rescue Dorothy. He wasn't about to go anywhere without her.

Of course, he had already created a small stir since he was captured outside the fence. Despite how careful he had been in the past, the Southern Marshal now knew he had found a way out. She would take extra steps to seal them in tighter than they were before.

Some leader he had turned out to be. He had just made it harder on all the hybrids in the compound. Any hope of escape in the near future had just been quelled. He was the last person they should be looking to for guidance.

But the Southern Marshal was right. From the moment he first arrived in the colony six months ago, everyone had looked to him as their leader. Rather than being treated as the new kid and shunned as a stranger, he was asked to sit in on the monthly council meetings. But as much as he tried to just sit there and remain silent, he was still called upon to settle disputes among the council members. And every decision he made immediately became law.

He was constantly being pulled by the hybrids within the colony to take a leadership position. Now he was being pushed from the outside, by the Southern Marshal herself, to do the same.

But a leader of what?

And where would he be leading the hybrids to?

He still had not figured out why the Southern Marshal had invited the hybrids to the Southern Territories. Why had she accumulated every hybrid into one place? What did she plan to do with them? Everyone he spoke to waved off his concerns and told him not to question their good fortune. Despite the electric fence, everyone told him, they were better off. Asking such questions would only invite trouble they didn't want to have.

His mind swirled over the same questions, for what seemed like hours, without coming to any new answers. Even without a window in the small room, he knew their journey was coming to an end. His ears popped as the airship descended. A final bump signaled that the airship had come to rest on the landing platform.

It was no surprise that, within five minutes of the airship landing, he heard the lock on the door to his small room engage and the door swung open. But it was a complete surprise when the first person who came through the door was Zee.

She placed balled fists on her hips and shook her head at him. "I told you. If you kept sneaking out, one day you would get caught."

"What are you doing here?"

She held up the cast iron key that would unlock the shackles on his hands. "I'm here to help you make the right decision."

"You told her I left as soon as I went through the fence, didn't you?"

She ignored his question and twisted the key in the lock. The shackles dropped free and he massaged his wrists, trying to bring blood flow back to his numb hands.

He couldn't believe Zee, who had become his closest friend in the colony, was working against him.

"How long have you been working for the Southern Marshal?"

She headed for the door when he grabbed her arm and forced her to look at him. "How could you do this to us?"

She met his stare. "There is no us. There is you, and there is the rest of the colony."

"What are you talking about?"

"Unlike you, we like the Southern Marshal. She has given back to the hybrids everything that humans took away from us. When you first arrived, I thought the colony was complete. You were supposed to usher in a new era for the hybrids. "

"What was your reward for turning me in?"

She broke free from his grasp. "There was no reward. I didn't turn you in. You got caught outside the fence all on your own. I had nothing to do with that."

"Then what are you doing here?"

She spoke so quietly with her head lowered, he missed what she said.

"What?"

This time she screamed it. "I'm here, we are all here, to watch you be crowned king. The council decided that, the biggest reason you are resisting your duties, is that there was no formal ceremony. We came here to make official what everyone has already accepted. And you don't deserve it!"

This was certainly news to him.

"What are you talking about? I'm not being crowned king."

"Yes, you are. I am here to help you get ready and to convince you it is the right thing to do. Even if I don't believe it myself."

This was getting all too surreal. "I don't deserve to be king."

"That is something we can both agree on. But it has already been decided. It is out of our hands."

"I can refuse."

She grew somber and spoke in a monotone as if she had practiced the same sentence over and over again.

"Then you will be executed for violating the rules of the colony. You only have two choices. Become the king or have your head chopped off by a Woodsman. I'm sure you can guess which one I prefer."

This was the first time Zee had ever been hostile toward him. This was not like her at all.

"What's the matter with you Zee?"

"There's nothing the matter with me. You're the problem. We finally have a place we can call our own and all you want to do is leave. You spent so much time away from your people, you don't even identify with them anymore."

"It has nothing to do with that, Zee. I have to find my friend."

She laughed. "That's right. Your little friend Dorothy. What can she offer you that none of us, who are your own people, can offer you?"

"It's not that. I made a promise to her."

"Yeah, well, your ancestors made a promise to my ancestors. And blood is thicker than water."

"What are you talking about? There are no ancestors. We are second-generation hybrids. Our parents were created in a lab."

Zee frowned. "Where did you hear nonsense like that?"

"It's not nonsense. It's the truth."

"You don't know anything about our history."

"That's because there is no history. We were deemed abominations of science and sent here to OZ to die."

She studied the ceiling for a moment before settling her eyes on his.

"I don't know what you were told, but our history has nothing to do with science.

Hybrids have been around for a very long time. We were the gods of long ago. Worshiped by the humans. Until they stole the Brahmastra, a weapon of immense power that could destroy anything you pointed it at. The humans used the Brahmastra to destroy the capital city of the hybrids. When they believed they had destroyed every one of us, they turned that weapon on each other. A few of our people survived and moved to a place where the humans could never reach them. Their plan was to wait for the humans to destroy themselves, and then we would be free to roam the world again. But with each passing century, humans didn't die out. Instead, they expanded into every corner of the world. It was getting harder and harder to stay hidden."

What she was telling him was absolutely unbelievable. Meaning, he did not believe a single word of it and wasn't about to listen to her spin fables from her childhood.

"Listen, Zee…"

She raised her hand and cut him off.

"Let me finish. Despite remaining hidden, we kept an eye on human advancements, and the evolution of their society. Fear and superstition had given way to logic and reason. All the ancient writings and depictions of our people were seen as fanciful attempts of prehistoric man trying to make sense of the world around him. My parents remember the day when the humans found us again. To explain why we looked part animal and part human, we said that we were test subjects in a genetics project. We felt that they would believe that more than if we told them we were the gods of their ancestors. And they did believe us. But the human's reaction was to outlaw genetic manipulation and send the hybrids here. My mother was pregnant with me when she was relocated to OZ. She told me these stories and made me promise to never forget them. Never forget the true history of our people."

Caleb thought her parents must've wanted to instill in her a sense of worth to offset the treatment of the hybrids by the humans in OZ. It's a shame they had manufactured an entire mythology, stretching back thousands of years, instead of having to explain that science had only recently created them. He could tell by the conviction set deep in her eyes that nobody would be able to convince her that what she just told him was anything but the truth.

"So, this is what you believe?"

"This is what we all believe, Caleb. Everybody but you."

"Then how come this is the first I've heard of it?"

"It's a rather hard pill to swallow if you've been fed the lie for as long as you have. We had hoped to tell you when you were ready. And we'd hoped you would be ready once you were crowned king."

"Why is it so important to everyone that I am the one crowned king?"

A new voice interrupted from the doorway. "I believe I can answer that one."

The Southern Marshal strode into the room. "Thank you, Zee. Why don't you go out and make sure everything is ready for the pre-coronation feast?"

Zee bowed low as she backed out of the room. Caleb noted how she did not stand up as long as she was still in view of the Southern Marshal. He assumed that as soon as she disappeared around the corner of the doorway, she stood up and went on her way.

"Still on that same old question are we?"

"You never gave me a straight answer before."

"I want you to be the king for the very same reasons they want you to be the king. "

"And what is that?"

"Because they will listen to you."

"That still doesn't answer why you want me to the king over the hybrids. What's in it for you?"

She studied him for a long time, her eyes darting back and forth in rapid succession as she waged a battle within her head. Finally she reached a hand into her mouth and pulled her teeth out.

With her false teeth removed, he could see the razor-sharp fangs that protruded longer than her shorter, but just as sharp, front teeth.

"Because I am one of you."

Chapter 7

The Southern Marshal replaced her false teeth back into her mouth. She shifted them with a twinge of her cheeks and once again looked entirely human. She examined him up and down with her eyes, appraising him.

"You look more like your mother than your father."

"You knew my parents?"

"Not very well. Being almost indistinguishable from human, I did not have much of a chance to speak with the king and queen. Prejudice is not strictly a human trait."

"Why have you kept that you are a hybrid a secret? By your reasoning, wouldn't they be more prejudiced against you thinking you're human?"

"There's no way I would've become the Southern Marshal if the humans knew what I was. I was not worried about being accepted by the hybrids as much as I needed to be accepted by the humans. Even before the humans found our hidden colony, there were still a select few we maintained contact with who were willing to trade with us without asking too many questions. I was passed off as human. Through me, the humans felt they could trust the hybrids, and since they believed I was a human myself, they did not kill me. Unfortunately, there is no one left who knows who I really am."

"If this is such a big secret, then why did you show me?"

"Because you have to know that we are all in this together. I'm not forcing you to do anything that I wouldn't gladly do myself. But I am not the sole living heir to the throne, you are. And I showed you because I wanted you to know that I have no ulterior motives toward the hybrids."

He didn't know how many more shocking revelations he could take in one day. He had finally received word that Dorothy might still be alive. He had seen the shadow of an airship that was invisible in the sky, and was now talking directly to the one person, who could not only give him Dorothy, but who had just revealed to him that she was a hybrid.

"Are there any more secrets you're keeping from me?"

"Just one."

"And what is it? I can take it."

"I'll leave it to someone else to tell you that secret. Come with me and I will take you to him."

"Why don't you tell me what it is?"

"I think it's better if you hear it from him. If anybody can convince you to follow the destiny of your birthright, he can."

Caleb didn't know how much more he could take in the trust department. There were too many secrets everywhere.

"Who are you taking me to?"

"If I told you that, you wouldn't meet with him."

"And how do you know that?"

She smiled. Her false teeth looked completely natural and completed the picture that she was fully human. "Because as much as you would like to think you have secrets too, Caleb. I can read you like an open book."

He opened his mouth to say something back, but drew a blank.

Her cloak flowed outward as she spiraled away from him and headed out the door. He glanced around at the bare walls and the single chain connected to the beam. He would not find any answers in here.

He followed her out of the airship and into her castle. They took several turns until she entered a small room. The room was dimly lit and a curtain filled one wall. She stood in the center room.

He glanced around, but the room was empty except for the two of them. The walls were bare and there was no furniture. The only thing different about the room was the curtain that filled the entire wall. The Southern Marshal stood facing the curtain as if anticipating it to open at any moment and reveal some great truth.

They stood there in silence until he couldn't take it any longer. "Are we waiting for the person I am to meet?"

"Not quite. There's something I would like to show you first. It might make you a little more motivated to hear what he has to say. Go ahead, pull back the curtain."

He looked at the large curtain and then back to the Southern Marshall. "What am I going to see?"

"You will see exactly what you want to see."

He barked out a laugh. "What? Is there some kind of magic mirror behind the curtain?"

"Pull it back and see."

He hesitated with his hand on the edge of the curtain.

The Southern Marshal stood silently waiting for him to make a decision. He let go of the edge of the curtain.

"And if I don't?"

"Then you will never know how close you came to getting what you want."

What he wanted was to get Dorothy back.

He looked at the big curtain that covered the entire wall. He had to take action to see what was on the other side. Nobody else would do it for him. He had to decide for himself if he felt ready for the unknown.

In a single action, he grabbed the curtain and yanked it back. His mouth gaped in surprise and his heart fluttered wildly.

Sitting in the room on the other side of the glass wall, which had previously been hidden by the curtain, was Dorothy.

She sat with her head bowed at a small table in the center of the room, her hands folded in her lap.

He ran up and banged on the glass wall with his fists. "Dorothy! Dorothy it's Caleb!"

Dorothy ignored him completely and kept her head half bowed.

He banged harder on the wall until his hands felt bruised. "Dorothy!"

The Southern Marshal was at his side. "She cannot hear you."

He pressed his forehead against the glass and watched Dorothy sitting peacefully on the other side. "Why have you shown me this?"

"I wanted you know that she is safe. And I want you to listen to what we have to say."

"I'm listening."

"Not me. You have to hear it from someone else."

She swept out of the room. The heels of her boots echoed back to him as she walked swiftly down the hall.

He took one last look at Dorothy and followed the Southern Marshal before she got too far. She held all the cards and she knew it. If he had any hope of getting Dorothy back, he would have to play along for a little while longer.

He followed her silently as they continued through her castle. They took so many turns, dark stairwells, both up and down, and went through several secret panel doors, he had no idea where he was anymore. He wasn't sure if they were even still inside the castle, or if they had traversed through underground caverns away from the castle grounds.

He hadn't seen a window, or any opening, to the outside for some time. They could have traveled a great distance or could, just as easily, be several feet from where they started.

She stopped at a small wooden door with no markings or decorations on it, save for a single brass handle.

"Beyond this door is the truth. Are you ready for it?"

The door was made from simple wooden planks and, except for the ornately carved brass handle, it was nondescript in every way. It's most important feature, Caleb noted, was the lack of a lock. At least, he could decide to leave anytime he wanted if he didn't like what he found on the other side of that door.

"Is the truth going to set me free?"

She grasped the handle. "I suspect it will do exactly the opposite."

She pushed the door open and motioned for him to step down into the dimly lit chamber. With each step he took down into the chamber, the temperature felt like it dropped several degrees. By the time he made it to the bottom step, it was at least twenty degrees cooler than when he first entered.

Back up the stairs, the Southern Marshal smiled down at him as she shut the door, plunging him into semi-darkness.

His feline eyes pierced the darkness and used the minimal light from strategically placed candles to resolve the room that stretched out before him.

A flare of light off to one side illuminated the face of the one man who always had a knack for showing up when he was least wanted. It was ironic that, deep down in this underground room, the only available light was born from fire. Much like the man before him had been reborn from fire.

Nero held the torch aloft in front of him as he walked past Caleb and used his torch to ignite others along one wall. He said nothing as he walked along the wall, lighting torches up one after the other.

Caleb could not bear the silence any longer.

"Let me guess. You're a hybrid too?"

Nero said nothing as he circled the room and ignited the last of the wall hanging torches. He had come full circle and stood in the same spot Caleb had seen him ignite the first torch. He placed the torch into the empty holder on the wall.

The front of the room was now brightly lit from both sides and Caleb could see that it was a large storage room. The floor was lined with a multitude of statues stretching off into the darkness, ancient looking scrolls were piled in neat stacks on wooden tables, and broken pieces of ornate carvings leaned against the walls. The room was filled with countless artifacts and treasures that blended into the darkness at the other end of the massive underground chamber.

Nero spread his arms, as if to encompass the entire room in his embrace.

"All those times that I traveled on extended business trips were actually spent here, sorting and cataloging all the artifacts we uncovered in OZ."

Nero lifted one of the scrolls off the table. "Nearly all the world's lost knowledge and history can be rediscovered in these scrolls here. All you need to do is learn a language that has been dead for thousands of years."

He neatly replaced the scroll at the top of the pile. "The answer to your question is no."

Caleb had been standing there silently listening to Nero. He didn't remember asking any question.

Nero noticed the look of confusion on his face and did his best to smile through the deep scars on his face.

"You asked if I was a hybrid. The answer is no. I was, however, born and raised among hybrids."

"That's not possible; the hybrids were created less than twenty years ago."

"Did you not listen to anything Zee told you?"

"Zee told me stories…"

Nero slammed his fist down on the table. "And every one of them true."

Caleb tugged at the hair of his mane in frustration. It seemed that lately, every time he turned around, somebody was spinning him a tale that conflicted with what he knew to be true his entire life.

"I'm sick of the lies."

The flickering of the torches made the shadows on Nero's scarred face dance, his face shimmering as if it had a life of its own.

"I agree, Caleb. No more lies. You have to know the truth because OZ, if not the entire world, depends on what you do next. And you can't make the right decision if you don't know the whole truth."

"And you expect me to believe that you will tell me the truth?"

"As much as I would like to, I can't force you to believe me. But I hope that for your sake, for all our sakes, you do."

"And why should I believe anything you say?"

"Because I promised your parents that I would look out for you and help you fulfill your destiny."

And so the lying began again. "Ha! You couldn't have promised my parents anything. You told me yourself you rescued me from my dying mother's arms right before some soldiers killed me."

"That part was true. Only, it didn't happen exactly in the way I told you."

Caleb shook his head in disgust. "Then why don't you enlighten me as to how it really happened."

"I told you that I was born and raised with hybrids. My closest friend was your father. Don't give me that look. You wanted the truth, so here it is.

"My mother and father were the only survivors of a shipwreck that washed them up onto the shore of an uncharted island. The hybrids found them and nursed them back to health, but kept them segregated from the colony. The ones who cared for my parents wore sackcloth over their entire body and hid the fact that they were part animal.

"As my parents recovered, they were encouraged to exercise but warned to stay close to their shelter and not venture into the forest. By accident, my mother became lost one day and wandered through the restricted area of the island and stumbled right into the middle of the hybrid colony.

"The hybrids had no intention of letting the world discover that they still existed, and thus could not let my mother go once she knew about them. The elders donned sackcloth to hide their animal appearance and approached my father. They told him my mother had broken the only rule given to them to obey and thus would not be allowed to leave the island. My father was given a choice. He could leave the island alone to rejoin civilization or be reunited with his wife and stay on the island forever.

"He chose to stay and it was on that island that I was born. The only human child among a colony of hybrids."

"This story is getting tedious."

"Patience Caleb. I just wanted you to know how close I was to your father. I was only a couple of years older than him and we grew up as brothers. Even before he became king, he knew it was only a matter of time before the humans found their island. They were spreading across the world and becoming more dangerous with each generation. He made me promise that, no matter what happened, I would do everything in my power to keep the colony safe.

"You were barely six months old when a small armada of three human ships found the island. Your father had just ascended to the throne and felt it was his duty to make first contact. He thought that by telling them the hybrids were a genetic experiment, they would show mercy. They did not. He was the first of many to die.

"I spent two weeks hiding you in different caves on the island, staying just ahead of the marauders. When they finally left and the fires died out, I found the bodies of those killed and gave them a proper burial. Including your mother and father."

"But it doesn't make sense. How could you have rescued me on the island at the same time you were supposedly rescuing me inside OZ?"

"The reason I was unable to save your parents from the three ships full of marauders was that I brought them to the island."

"What!? Why?"

"Your grandfather took full advantage of the fact that I was human and sent me out to infiltrate a group they believed knew the location of the ancient source of the hybrid's power. A small clandestine group, calling themselves the Directors, was searching for the Brahmastra, an ancient artifact that would enable them to conquer the world. Part of the ancient texts they were using in their search made mention of the hybrids. I let my guard down for the briefest of moments and let slip that I already knew about animal-human hybrids. They made me tell them where the island was."

Caleb was staring into the face of pure evil. This man had lied to him his entire life and, when he finally told the truth, he admitted to being directly responsible for the death of his parents.

"So you gave up my parents, the whole colony, just like that?"

"They were… very persuasive."

"All this time, you made me believe you saved me when, the whole time, you were the one who killed my parents."

"I didn't kill them."

"But you led the humans right to them, knowing what would happen."

"I'm sorry, Caleb. But it's time you knew the truth."

"Why?"

"Because there's something you need to do…"

"No! Not that. Why did you betray my parents?"

Nero paused and looked deep into Caleb's eyes, as if willing him to believe what he was about to say.

"I did not betray your parents."

He had had enough of this. It was impossible to know if any of this was the truth. For all he knew, these could be all new lies hiding an even worse truth. Caleb shook his head and headed up the stairs. Away from the man who killed his parents. Away from the lies.

Nero called after him. "What I did may have resulted in the death of your parents, yes. But I did it under specific orders from the king at the time I was sent out. Your grandfather gave me explicit instructions to find out how close the humans were to finding the hybrid weapon."

Caleb pushed on the door, but it bumped against something heavy resting against it on the other side. He pushed harder, but his feet slid on the floor and the door refused to budge any further.

He headed back down the stairs as Nero continued. "Your parents knew what was at stake."

Caleb peered into the darkness at the other end of the underground warehouse. "Is there another door down there?"

"The group your grandfather sent me to infiltrate was getting closer to finding the Brahmastra. A weapon used at various times throughout history by different groups to conquer their known world. Its whereabouts was unknown for over a thousand years until an archaeological expedition, financed by the

Directors, uncovered evidence of its final resting place."

Caleb grabbed a torch off the wall and made his way through the haphazardly placed artifacts and into the darkness of the ever-deepening warehouse. Nero shuffled along quickly behind him.

"I had the Brahmastra in my hands only two days ago, but due to circumstances beyond my control, I lost it again. That would not be so bad if it weren't for the armada of one thousand airships, each filled with soldiers, landing in OZ in less than a week. They will destroy everything in their path until they have the Brahmastra. We cannot let that happen. You cannot let that happen."

He continued on as straight a path as he could, but every step he took only revealed that the warehouse stretched even further into the darkness; the far wall always staying just out of reach of the flame from his torch. The flickering fire cut an arc through the air as he turned on Nero.

"Your little story is very interesting, but I've had enough earth shattering revelations for today. How do I get out of here?"

Nero panted from the exertion of trying to keep up with him.

"You have to find the Brahmastra and destroy it."

"I don't have to do anything. I promised to listen to you and then I could decide for myself what I wanted to do. I want to leave."

"But what about your destiny?"

"What destiny? I'm nothing but a casino enforcer, thanks to you. I am not some great hero for the hybrids. I've been told I can leave after listening to you, and that's exactly what I intend to do. And I want to take Dorothy with me."

Nero shook his head. "I'm sorry. If you want to leave, fine. But you will do so alone."

He leaned in close to Nero, the torch illuminating both their faces in the darkness. "When I come back for Dorothy, I will not be alone."

The Adventure Continues...

Sign up for Steve's Book Report (Mailing List) @ SteveDW.com
Know when his next book is released and other trouble he gets into ;-)

Other Books by the Author

A is for Apprentice (Fantasy)

Oliver Twist: Victorian Vampire (Fantasy)

A Tale of Two Cities with Dragons (Fantasy)

Shade Infinity (Science Fiction Thriller)

Peacekeepers X-Alpha Series (Thriller)
    Inherit the Throne
    The Warrior's Code

Steampunk OZ Series (Science Fiction Serial)
    Forgotten Girl

The Legacy's World

Emerald Shadow

The Future's Destiny

The Dangerous Captive

Missing Legacy

Shadow of History

The Edge of the Hunter

Fugue: The Cure (Science Fiction Short Story)

Stay informed about all the trouble I keep getting into. Subscribe to Steve DeWinter's Book Report (i.e. the mailing list) @ SteveDW.com

www.ingramcontent.com/pod-product-compliance
Lightning Source LLC
Chambersburg PA
CBHW021100130626
46552CB00005B/2194